PIPPA'S
PASSOVER PLATE

PIPPA'S PASSOVER PLATE

by Vivian Kirkfield
illustrated by Jill Weber

Holiday House • New York

Hurry, scurry,

Pippa Mouse,

washing,

scrubbing,

cleaning house.

Passover starts at six tonight,
Seder meal by candlelight.

Hustle, bustle, lots to do.

Pippa stirs a chicken stew.

Sets the table—all looks great.

Where's the special Seder plate?

HAGGADAH

HAGGADAH

Pippa searches in a bin,
finds her missing rolling pin.

Pippa opens up a box,
filled with eighteen holey socks.

Pippa climbs up on a chair,
stretches up—the cupboard's bare!

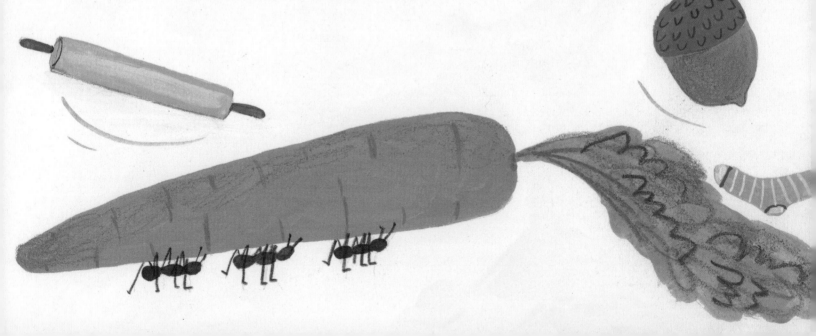

PASSOVER

CHICKEN
STEW

MATZOS

CARROTS

Teeter-totter—hold on tight!
Weeble-wobble—what a fright!

MATZOS

MATZOS

Pippa runs out to the yard.

Sphinx, the cat, is standing guard.

QUIVER! QUAVER!
SHIVER! SHAKE!

Cats make Pippa cringe and quake.

Pippa, though afraid to stir,
gently strokes the velvet fur.
"Have you seen my Seder plate?
Sun sets soon—it's getting late."

"No," purrs Cat.
"Go ask the snake,
slither-sliding
near the lake."

**QUIVER!
SHIVER!**

**QUAVER!
SHAKE!**

Snakes make Pippa cringe and quake.

Pippa scrambles down the lane.
Offers Snake a daisy chain.
"Have you seen my Seder plate?
Sun sets soon—it's getting late."

"No, I haven't," Snake replies.
"Go ask Owl, she's old and wise."

QUIVER!   QUAVER!
SHIVER!   SHAKE!

Owls make Pippa cringe and quake.

Stumble, tumble down the trail.
Pippa prays she will not fail.

In a quiet woodland glade,
Owl sits in leafy shade.

"Have you seen my Seder plate?
Sun sets soon—it's getting late."
"No, I haven't seen the dish.
Why not question Golda Fish?"

Golda loves to primp and preen.
She was once a beauty queen.
Seder plate is made of brass,
shining like a looking glass.

At the water, near the edge,
Pippa climbs up on a hedge.
Thinks she spies a golden fin...
Splash! Poor mouse has fallen in!

At the bottom—
something round.

Can you guess what Pippa found?

Ball and coin and old tin can,
bottle cap and rusty pan,
globe to circumnavigate.
Best of all—the Seder plate!

Fish swims up with mouse in tow.
To the Seder all will go.

Pippa and the others cheer.
Life is good when friends are near.

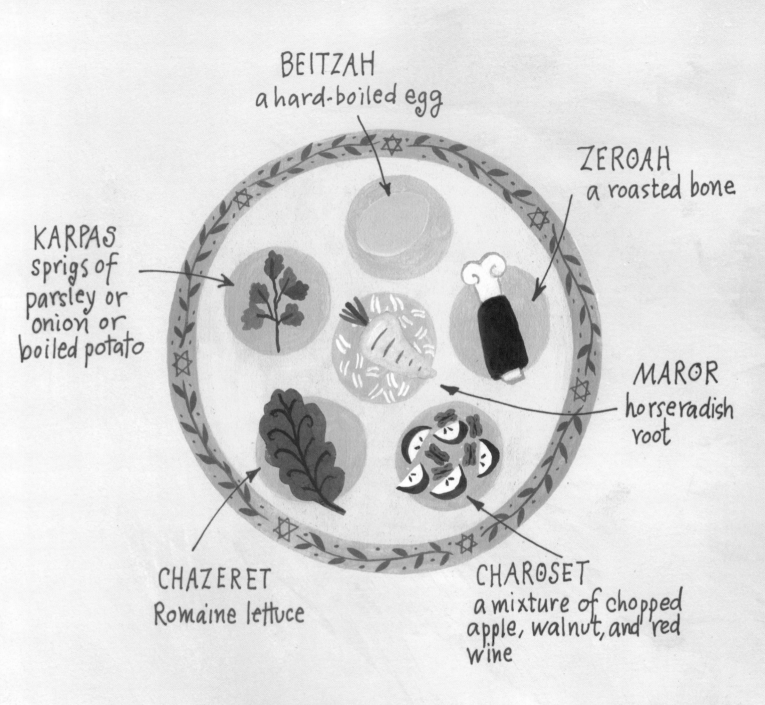

BEITZAH
a hard-boiled egg

ZEROAH
a roasted bone

KARPAS
sprigs of
parsley or
onion or
boiled potato

MAROR
horseradish
root

CHAZERET
Romaine lettuce

CHAROSET
a mixture of chopped
apple, walnut, and red
wine

SEDER PLATE

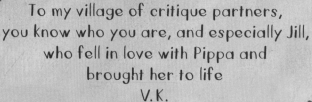

To my village of critique partners,
you know who you are, and especially Jill,
who fell in love with Pippa and
brought her to life
V.K.

For Rainer, Sterling, Jack
& Charlotte
J.W.

Text Copyright © 2019 by Vivian Kirkfield
Illustrations Copyright © by Jill Weber
All Rights Reserved
HOLIDAY HOUSE is registered in the U.S. Patent and Trademark Office.
Printed and bound in October 2018 at Toppan Leefung, DongGuan City, China.
The artwork for this book was created with acrylic gouache and Neocolor crayons with a bit of collage.
www.holidayhouse.com
First Edition
1 3 5 7 9 10 8 6 4 2

Library of Congress Cataloging-in-Publication Data
is available on the Library of Congress website.

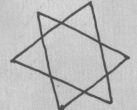

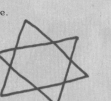
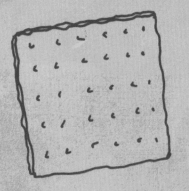